Animal Doctors

What Do They Do?

by CARLA GREENE

Pictures by
LEONARD KESSLER

SCHOLASTIC BOOK SERVICES

NEW YORK • TORONTO • LONDON • AUCKLAND • SYDNEY

Text copyright © 1967 by Carla Greene. Pictures copyright © 1967 by Leonard Kessler. This edition is published by Scholastic Book Services, a division of Scholastic Magazines, Inc., by arrangement with Harper & Row, Publishers, Incorporated.

1st printing...November 1969
Printed in the U.S.A.

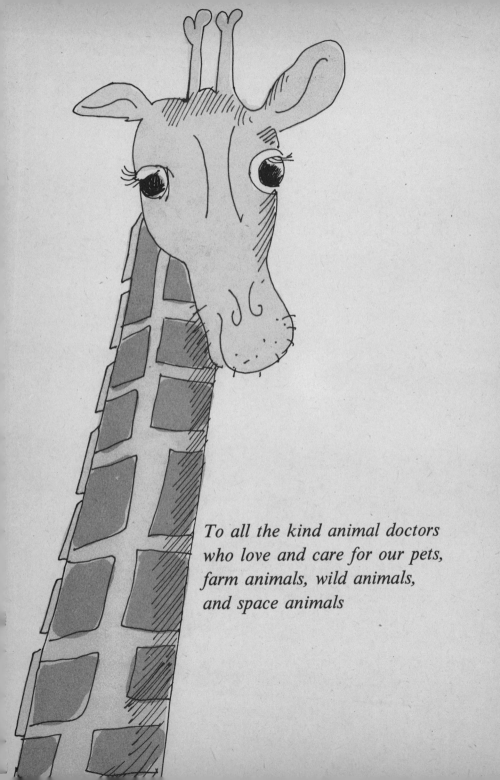

*To all the kind animal doctors
who love and care for our pets,
farm animals, wild animals,
and space animals*

Words to learn about

microscope

X ray

splint

veterinarian

animal doctors

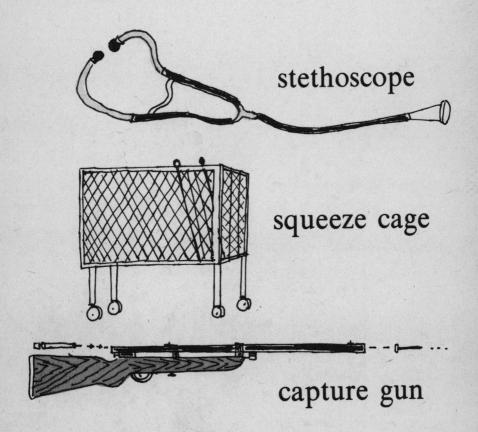

stethoscope

squeeze cage

capture gun

ambulance

Do you have a pet?

A dog or a cat? A hamster?

A snake or a lizard?

A canary or a parakeet?

If you have any kind of pet,
you may know
an animal doctor.

It takes a long time
to become an animal doctor.
An animal doctor goes to college
for at least six years.

He learns about many kinds
of animals, reptiles, and birds.
He learns about animal foods
and medicines.

He looks into a microscope and sees
the germs that make animals sick.

He learns to take X rays
to see if an animal has broken bones.

He learns to set broken bones
so they will mend.

Some animal doctors live
in the city.
They take care of city pets.

Some animal doctors live
in the country.
They take care of farm animals
and country pets.

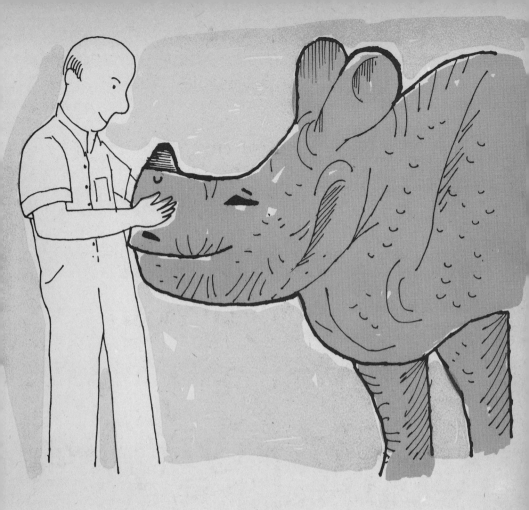

Some animal doctors take care
of wild animals in a zoo or circus.

A few animal doctors
look after animals
that are sent into outer space.

THE CITY ANIMAL DOCTOR

Johnny has a pet dog named Frisky.
Frisky will not eat or play.

"Frisky must be sick,"
says Johnny's mother. "Let's take him
to the veterinarian."

"What is a veterinarian?" asks Johnny.

"He is an animal doctor," says Mother.

Johnny and Mother take Frisky
to see Doctor Smith.
The doctor's waiting room is full
of people with their pets.

"Down, Horace! Down!" cries Mary.
Her monkey is swinging
on the hat rack.

"Hush, Polly! Hush!" says Grandma
to her noisy parrot.

"No, no! No fighting, Tom!"
scolds Billy,
holding tightly on to his cat.

Doctor Smith takes care of the pets
one after the other.

Polly's wing is broken.
The doctor puts a splint on it.

Billy's fighting cat has a cut eye.
The doctor puts medicine on it.

Mary's monkey is not sick.
He only needs a shot
to keep him from getting sick.

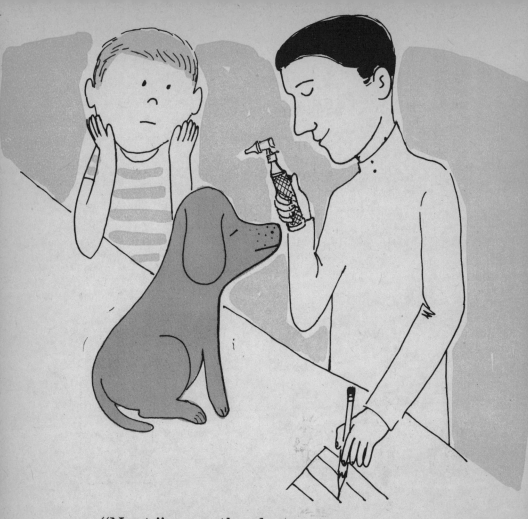

"Next," says the doctor.

Now it is Frisky's turn.
Doctor Smith puts Frisky on a table.
He listens to Frisky's heart.
He looks into Frisky's eyes and mouth.

"Frisky needs an operation,"
says the doctor.
"He had better stay in my hospital
for a few days. Come, Johnny,
I will show you the hospital."

So many cages! So many kinds
of animals in the cages!

"Here is a nice cage for Frisky,"
says the doctor.

Johnny feels sad, but he leaves Frisky
in Doctor Smith's hospital.

Doctor Smith has a helper named Sally.
Sally takes care of the hospital.

She gives the animals their food.
She gives them the medicines
which Doctor Smith has ordered.
She keeps the cages neat and clean.

In the morning and evening
Doctor Smith visits the animals
in the hospital.

The next day Doctor Smith
operates on Frisky.

Doctor Smith puts Frisky to sleep.
Frisky does not feel anything.

Soon the operation is over.
In a few days Frisky is well again.

Johnny comes to take Frisky home.
Frisky jumps up on Johnny.
He is so glad to see him!

Doctor Smith is glad too.
He is always happy when he makes
an animal well.

THE COUNTRY ANIMAL DOCTOR

Doctor Jones lives in the country.

He is an animal doctor.

Cock-a-doodle-doo!

Cock-a-doodle-doo!

Early in the morning

the rooster crows.

It is time for Doctor Jones

to start his day.

25

Doctor Jones must drive from farm
to farm to see the animals.
He can take care of an animal
in a farmer's barn.

Doctor Jones must often wade
through water, so he wears overalls
and high rubber boots.

He carries some of the things he needs
in his black bag
and some in the trunk of his car:

medicines and pills,

bandages,

a stethoscope,

a needle for shots,

a thermometer,

a small X-ray machine,
and other things.

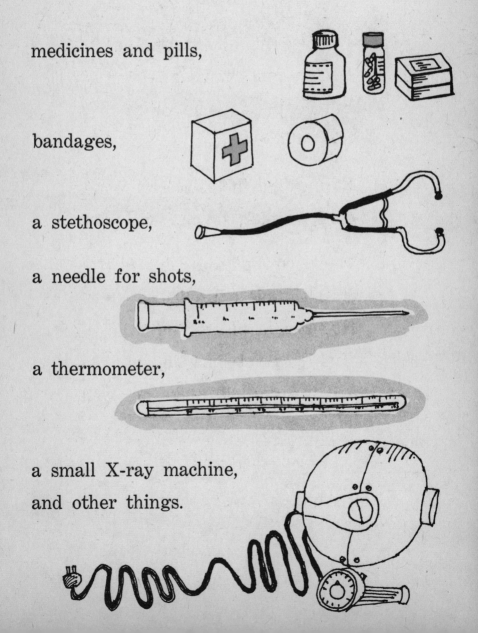

Farmer Bill's horse, Jennie, is sick.
Doctor Jones must give her a pill.
But Jennie does not want
to swallow a pill.

Farmer Bill helps Doctor Jones
open Jennie's strong jaws.

The doctor puts a tube
down Jennie's throat.
He blows a pill through the tube.
This does not hurt Jennie,
and the pill will make her well.

Oink! Oink!
Farmer Bill's pig
does not want to eat.
She *must* be sick!

Doctor Jones examines her.
He takes out his needle
and gives her a shot.
The pig squeals for a moment,
but soon she will be eating again.

Doctor Jones has a telephone
in his car.

Ring, ring, ring!
The doctor's wife is calling.
"Go to the Nelson farm right away,"
says the doctor's wife.

Off to the Nelson farm he goes.
He gets there just in time
to take care of a new baby calf.

Day after day Doctor Jones
drives miles and miles
over bumpy country roads,
in heat or cold, rain or snow.

The farmers and their animals
could not get along
without Doctor Jones.

THE ZOO ANIMAL DOCTOR

CITY ZOO
ANIMAL HOSPITAL
DR. J. ADAMS D.V.M.
VETERINARIAN

Doctor Adams is the animal doctor
in a large city zoo.
He has a hospital at the zoo.
He rides around in his ambulance and
visits the animals, reptiles, and birds.

Roar! Roar! Looey, the lion, walks
around and around in his cage.
Looey's head hangs down and
he swings it from side to side.

"Looey has a headache,"
says the doctor to the zookeeper.
"I must give Looey a shot."

Looey looks angry.

It is not safe to go into his cage.

How can the doctor give Looey a shot?

The zookeeper brings a small cage.
It is called a *squeeze cage*.
He puts some meat in the squeeze cage.

Quick, quick!
The zookeeper opens the door
of Looey's cage, and puts
the open squeeze cage next to it.

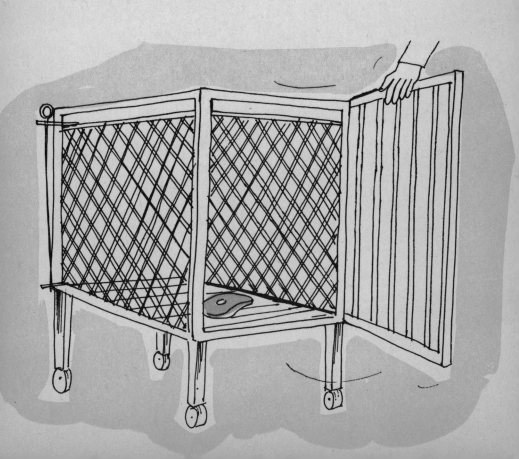

Looey goes after the meat.

Quick, quick!
The zookeeper closes the door
of the squeeze cage.

The small cage fits close
to Looey's body,
but it does not hurt him.

Now the doctor can come
close to Looey
and give him a shot in the hip.
Looey will soon be well again.

Bennie, the big moose,

needs his hoofs trimmed.

He runs around in the deer park.

It is hard to catch him.

Doctor Adams gets his *capture gun*.

The gun does not shoot bullets.

It shoots a needle
with medicine in it.

The medicine puts Bennie to sleep
for a little while.
Now the doctor
can trim Bennie's hoofs.

The zookeeper calls Doctor Adams.
"Come quickly!
Mandy, the elephant, has a fever!"

Doctor Adams jumps into his ambulance
and rushes to Mandy.

"I will give Mandy some medicine
in her favorite food —
chocolate ice cream,"
says the doctor.

Doctor Adams puts the medicine
in a pail of chocolate ice cream.
But he does not fool Mandy.

She fills her trunk with ice cream,
then . . .

Squirt! Squirt!
Doctor Adams is covered with chocolate.

"Too bad, Mandy," says the doctor.
"Now I will have to give you a shot."

Mandy has to be chained
to make her stand still.
But her hide is so thick
she does not feel the prick of the needle.
The next day Mandy is much better.

The zoo animal doctor keeps very busy.

In one day he may take care of

a nervous, spitting camel,

an angry anteater,

a sick scaly snake,

a growling tiger,
and almost any other animal.
How many can you think of?

THE CIRCUS ANIMAL DOCTOR

Doctor Black is the animal doctor
in a circus.
He watches the animals carefully.
They must stay well
so they can do their tricks!

Around and around the circus ring
go the beautiful prancing horses.

Oh, dear!
The bareback rider's horse falls.
Doctor Black takes the horse
out of the ring.

He X-rays her leg.

Thank goodness it is only a sprain!

The doctor bandages the horse's leg.

She must stay out of the ring

until her leg heals.

Doctor Black takes care
of wild circus animals too.
A lion has a broken jaw.
Doctor Black must mend it.

A giraffe has
a sore throat.
Up a ladder
goes the doctor
to look into
the giraffe's throat.

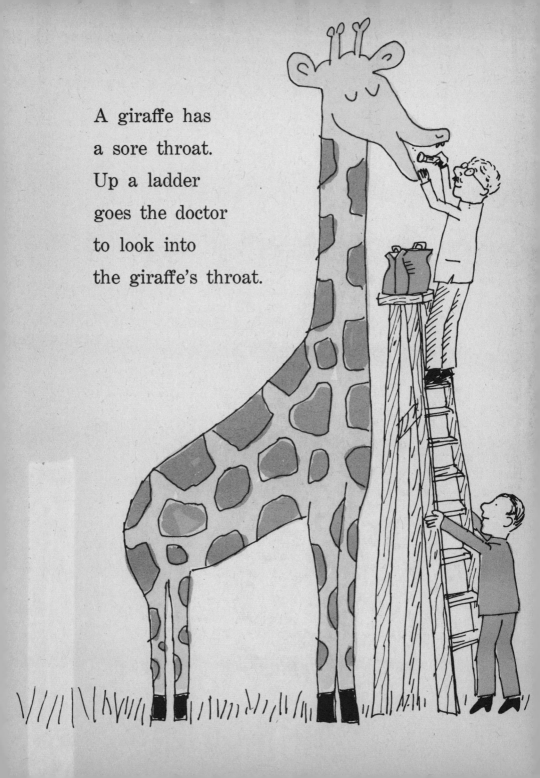

A mother gorilla and her baby
need the doctor's help.
The doctor is right there!

One day Pedro, the bear trainer,
brings Grizzly, the dancing bear,
to Doctor Black's hospital.

"Oh, my! Oh, my!" Pedro wails.
"Grizzly has a sore foot.
He cannot dance. My act is spoiled.
Oh, what can I do?"

Doctor Black looks at Grizzly's foot.

"He only has a splinter,"
says the doctor.

He pulls the splinter out
and puts medicine on Grizzly's foot.
Soon Grizzly is dancing again.

Roar! Roar!

Gr-rr-rr! Gr-rr-rr! Gr-rr-rr!

A hurt or sick wild animal

is often very dangerous.

Sometimes the animal doctor must risk

his life to make the animal well.

The zoo or circus animal doctor

is very brave!

THE SPACE ANIMAL DOCTOR

Ten, nine, eight, seven, six, five,
four, three, two, one, zero —
BLAST-OFF!

The astronauts take off into space.
We are almost sure
they will come back safely.
Why do we think so?

Because a monkey has made the flight
before the men try it.

The monkey is trained
by a team of scientists.
While the monkey is being trained,
a space animal doctor examines
and tests him again and again.

The doctor tests the monkey's heart,
his temperature, his breathing,
his brain, and his muscle actions.

The doctor can tell how
a man will feel in outer space
by the way the monkey acts.

Here is Ham, the famous space chimp.
Ham was trained to fly
in a space capsule
and return safely to earth.

While Ham was training,
the doctor tested and examined him
over and over again.
The doctor and Ham
became good friends.

At last, one day Ham blasted off
into outer space.

Many people waited to welcome Ham
back from his flight.

Hooray! Hooray! He landed safely.
What do you think Ham did first?

He reached out and shook hands
with his friend,
the space animal doctor.